For Jenny

SIMON & SCHUSTER BOOKS FOR YOUNG READERS
An imprint of Simon & Schuster Children's Publishing Division
1230 Avenue of the Americas, New York, New York 10020
First published in Great Britain in 2001 by Hodder Children's Books,
a division of Hodder Headline Limited
First U.S. edition, 2001
SIMON & SCHUSTER BOOKS FOR YOUNG READERS
is a trademark of Simon & Schuster.
The text for this book is set in 18-point AdLib.
Printed in Hong Kong
2 4 6 8 10 9 7 5 3 1
Library of Congress Control Number: 2001087719
ISBN 0-689-84695-9

FRANKENSTEIN'S CAT

Curtis Jobling

Simon & Schuster Books for Young Readers
New York London Toronto Sydney Singapore

Now, we all know the story of Frankenstein and his monster. Frank was a misunderstood, some would say mad, doctor, who made a man out of body parts. Monster goes mad, lots of tears, end of story.

   Well, the monster wasn't the doctor's first experiment.

   There was another.

Meet Frankenstein's cat. Kind of funny looking, isn't he?

The doctor named him Nine.

Not because cats have "nine lives," but because that's how many cats it took to make him. A Persian here, a Siamese there, a couple of tabbies, a few mousers, and a
very,
very,
very smelly alley cat
thrown in for good measure.

Well, life was never going to be easy for a cat that looked (and smelled) like that. The folks who lived in the castle liked things that were just plain ordinary and, clearly, Frankenstein's cat was no ordinary cat.

But Nine was determined to make some friends. With a stinky spring in his stuttering stride, he visited the castle kitchen.

The sweet smell of baking pastries attracted him like a bee to honey. Frankenstein's cat slinked up to the cook and rubbed up against her legs.

"Pee-yew!" exclaimed the cook, pinching her nose. "What is that awful smell?"

"Only me," said Nine. "Can I help?"

"Yes," said Cook. "You can start by getting your smelly paws out of my kitchen. Be off with you!"

After a swift swipe from Cook's broom, Frankenstein's cat scampered away.

"I know," he thought. "I'll try the courtyard. I bet I'll find a friend there." He hopped into the yard, where he bumped into some village children playing.

"Can I join in?" asked Nine.

"Yuck! What is that smell!" all the children muttered.

One boy stepped up—not too close.

"We're playing hide-and-seek," he said. "Sure you can join in. Go and hide!"

Frankenstein's cat bounded off excitedly and hid behind a tree.

Once there, he waited. And waited.

And waited.

"What's happened to them?" he thought. "They should have found me by now; I'm not even that well hidden!"

Only when he got up and looked for them did he spot them playing in a faraway field. With a sigh and a sniff, he went back into the castle.

In the hall, he found the butler, spring-cleaning the castle.

Nine skidded up to his feet, tail swishing excitedly and only occasionally falling off.

"Please, Mr. Butler, can I help you with the cleaning? I promise I'll do a good job. Please, please!"

Curling up his nose, the butler looked him up and down.

"Hmmm. I suppose so. I can't really see what trouble you can cause."

That was the butler's big mistake.

Twenty minutes, lots of chaos, and plenty of broken dishes later, Frankenstein's cat was shown the exit.

"It's not my fault my limbs have a life of their own! I didn't choose them," he grumbled.

"Out!" shouted the butler, pointing to the door.

Fed up, Frankenstein's cat went to the doctor's laboratory, where his master was hard at work.

"It's no good," said Nine. "I'm lonely and I need a friend."

He shuffled about on his mismatched feet before settling by the fire.

That's when he had his idea (he didn't have many so this was quite a special occasion).

He looked up at the doctor with bright eyes (well, one was bright, the other was a bit dull!). "Make me a companion, Master! Please?"

And so the doctor set to work.

As the doctor chopped and sewed, stitched and sawed, Nine paced back and forth anxiously, nervous as a newborn kitten (something he'd never actually been!).

"Oh, boy," he thought. "A friend! I can't wait!"

His thoughts were interrupted by his master's voice.

"Enter!" the doctor called,
and Frankenstein's cat rushed in.

He saw a shape, draped in a white sheet, lying on the doctor's operating table. As a storm rumbled overhead and lightning lit up the laboratory, the doctor pulled hard on a huge metal lever.

Electricity coursed along cables to the body on the table. Slowly, but surely, it began to twitch and shudder.

The figure sat upright, the sheet still covering it. The doctor stepped up and grabbed the edge of the sheet, a warm smile spread across his face.

"Frankenstein's cat," said the doctor, pulling the sheet away,

"meet Fifi . . ."

"... Frankenstein's dog!"

The cat felt sick.

With a screech of horror, Frankenstein's cat jumped four feet into the air, legs whirring, before turning tail and sprinting for the door. Frankenstein's dog replied with a bellowing "Woof!" before lurching after him on his clumsy paws.

And that is how our sorry story ends, with Frankenstein's dog chasing Frankenstein's cat around the castle for forever and a day! If one had to come up with a moral to this story—and I'm not sure there is one—I guess it could be this:

What you get (in this case a large, vicious zombie dog) isn't always what you asked for.

Just bear that in mind when you
ask for a puppy for a present!